Recorder

for beginners

Contents

CD recorded at Bar None Studios, Northford, CT

An Easy Beginning Method

Copyright © MMI by Alfred Music

All rights reserved. Produced in USA.
ISBN 0-7390-1100-6 (Book)
ISBN 0-7390-1101-4 (Book & CD)
ISBN 0-7390-1102-2 (CD)

Cover painting: Giraudon/Art Resource, NY
16th century Italian school, "The Pastoral Concert: Music"
Museé de l'Hotel Lallemant, Bourges, France.

On the front cover, the recorder player is using an antiquated playing position, which reverses the left and right hands from the correct modern position as used in this book.

SUSAN LOWENKRON

About the Author

Susan Lowenkron is a graduate of the Eastman School of Music and holds a master's degree from the Hartt School of Music. She presently teaches at the Hartford Conservatory of Music and Dance and at the Thames Valley Music School at Connecticut College.

Active as a performer throughout New England and New York, she is the founder and director of TAPESTRY, a trio playing Medieval, Renaissance and Baroque chamber music as well as traditional folk dance music from the British Isles and Eastern Europe. A 1972 winner of the Bodky Award for Early Music with the Boston-based RENAISSANCE CONSORT, she plays flutes, recorders, krummhorn, whistles and harp.

At the Hartford Conservatory, she is the director of the student ensemble program and coordinator of student recitals. As a teacher, she has given recorder workshops for the Eastern Connecticut Recorder Society in Connecticut, New Hampshire, New York and Vermont, and for the American Recorder Society.

Acknowledgements

Thanks to all of my students from whom I learn how and what to teach, to Nat Gunod for his expert and supportive assistance, and to the staff of the Hartford Conservatory for their much-needed computer advice. Thanks to Laura Mazza-Dixon for brightening up the CD with her guitar accompaniment.

Dedication

I dedicate this book to my husband, also a musician, whose patience was invaluable, and who gave up his side of the couch to all of my writing materials.

Track 00

A compact disc is available for this book. This disc can make learning with this book easier and more enjoyable. This symbol will appear next to every example that is on the CD. Use the CD to help insure that you are capturing the feel of the examples, interpreting the rhythms correctly, and so on. The track numbers below the symbols correspond directly to the example you want to hear. Have fun!

Introduction

The goal of this book is to share the joy and rewards of making music. It will teach you the basic skills for playing the soprano recorder, even if you do not read music or have never played an instrument before. Whether you are a young person or an adult beginner, this book can be used as an independent study guide to making music on one of the oldest woodwind instruments. My intent is to give you a sense of involvement and achievement right from the start. Already, in Chapter 1, you will be playing "real" music—folk songs, familiar hymns, oldies-but-goodies and real oldies from the recorder's golden days of the Renaissance and Baroque periods.

I have introduced new notes, pieces and concepts progressively, so it is best to use the book in the order given. By the end of the book, you will have learned more than fifteen notes, several time and key signatures and many musical symbols and terms. I feel that you will learn the notes better by writing them yourself, so composition exercises have been included; this will also give you a clearer idea of what makes a piece "work," and best of all, you can be creative.

As with all instrumental training, playing the recorder is far more than putting the correct finger down on the correct hole at the correct time. Hopefully, with your careful listening (and my little reminders), the ideas of good tonguing and tone, correct breathing and attention to musical phrases can also be a part of your music making.

The recorder is a serious musical instrument with a rich and varied repertoire. It is my hope to inspire you to go further in your musical studies, explore the possibilities of playing in recorder ensembles and investigate the other sizes of this family of instruments.

Have fun!

History of the Recorder

For more than 900 years, nobility and common people alike have enjoyed the instrument that you are about to start playing. The name "recorder" comes from the Old English verb "to record," which meant "to warble or sing like a bird." One of its names in French, *flute douce*, refers to the gentle sound of the instrument ("sweet flute"). Another French name for the recorder, *flute a bec*, is based on its appearance ("beaked flute"). The name in Italian, *flauto dirrito*, tells us about its playing position ("straight flute"). The German name, *blockflöte*, deriving from its whistle-type mouthpiece, is a clue to its construction.

Artwork showing recorders dates back to the 12th century. King Henry VIII owned 70 of them 400 years later and they were a familiar sound at theaters of Shakespeare's time. By the early 17th century, noted German composer and arranger Michael Praetorius, listed as many as nine sizes of recorders, ranging from the *sopranino* (smaller than the soprano) to the *contra-bass*. Famous composers of the Baroque era such as Bach, Handel and Vivaldi wrote brilliantly for professional recorder players of their time. The recorder often appears in folk music settings, and today's composers have made use of its special tonal qualities in jazz, film scores and even in Broadway tunes.

The recent resurgence of interest in early music and the recorder and its music has inspired an ever-growing number of instrument makers, amateur and professional soloists and ensembles to include recorders. The recorder-in-the-schools program is alive and well, and the number of universities that offer a major in recorder performance is also on the rise. It is a good time to be learning this instrument.

Chapter 1

Your Soprano Recorder

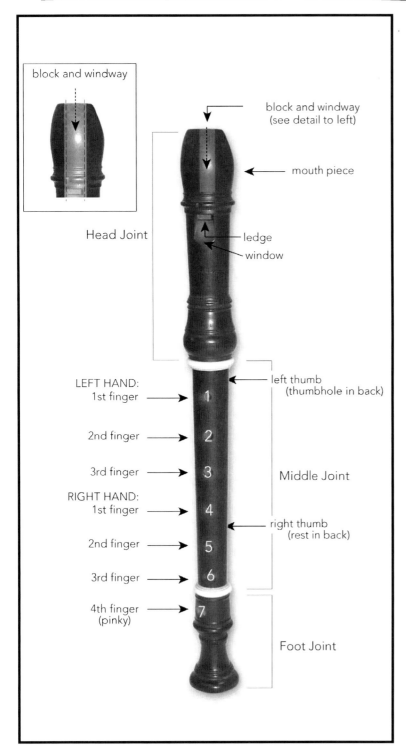

block and windway

Head Joint

block and windway
(see detail to left)

mouth piece

ledge

window

LEFT HAND:
1st finger → 1

2nd finger → 2

3rd finger → 3

RIGHT HAND:
1st finger → 4

2nd finger → 5

3rd finger → 6

4th finger
(pinky) → 7

left thumb
(thumbhole in back)

Middle Joint

right thumb
(rest in back)

Foot Joint

Recorder Construction

Recorders are made of either plastic or wood and have three parts: the head joint, the middle joint and the foot joint. On some instruments these three parts are not detachable. On the two- and three-piece construction, the player has the most flexibility to rotate the foot joint for the best location of the pinky finger.

Recorder Care

Both plastic and wooden instruments need to adjust to room and body temperature before being played to avoid a quick build-up of moisture in the windway, causing a "froggy" tone. To warm it, you can either cover the mouthpiece with your hand or put it under your arm for about a minute.

When the tone does get fuzzy (as it will eventually), you can unclog the windway either by

- sucking your breath in quickly with your mouth on the mouthpiece, or
- putting your index finger across the ledge of the window (but not touching the slanted area) and giving a few strong blows.

It is also a good idea to repeat this procedure before putting your instrument away.

The diagram below shows the number names of the fingers.

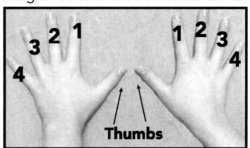

This diagram shows how to read the recorder fingering diagrams used in this book.

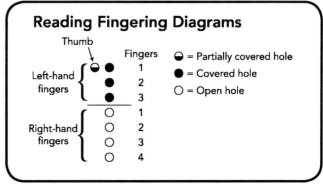

Reading Fingering Diagrams

Thumb

Fingers

Left-hand
fingers

1
2
3

Right-hand
fingers

1
2
3
4

◐ = Partially covered hole
● = Covered hole
○ = Open hole

Beginning to Play

1. Pick up your recorder with your right hand near the bottom of the instrument.

2. Cover the thumbhole in the back with your left thumb, still holding the recorder near the bottom.

3. Now put the 1st finger of your left hand on the 1st hole at the top. (Your thumb is still covering the back thumbhole.)

4. Let the recorder rest gently on your right thumb. It should be behind hole 5, while the other right-hand fingers stay slightly above, but not covering, holes 5, 6 and 7.

Correct Hand Position

These photographs show how your fingers should look when all of the holes are covered. Notice that we use the pads of the fingers and the fingers not being used, the left-hand pinky in this case, are kept in a loose, curled position.

The diagram below shows your current fingering. The thumbhole and hole 1 are covered.

5. Place the recorder on the dry part of your lower lip in *front* of your teeth. Gently close your mouth on the mouthpiece. It is important that your teeth and your tongue do not touch this part of the recorder.

6. Take a breath without raising your shoulders, and breathe gently into the recorder, starting the air with a silent "tu" (if you think of a "t" word such as "tuna," you'll find that the tip of your tongue starts a "tu" on the roof of your mouth). Think "blow light, hold tight." Your first tone! It should be a low sound, if you follow the "blow light, hold tight" idea. Feel the rims of the holes with the pads of your fingers. Every note has a letter name. The note you are playing is called B.

7. Try playing several Bs in a row. Remember to *tongue* ("tu") each note gently. Blowing too hard can cause high squeaks; so can finger leaks (not covering a hole completely).

You're ready to play!

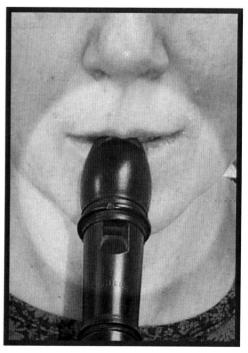

Correct Mouth Position

6

On this page, you'll learn your first recorder exercises. One of the most important aspects of playing music is keeping time. Musical time, or *rhythm*, is measured in beats, which are like a musical heartbeat. We strive to keep the beats pulsing evenly.

In written music, we organize beats into groups called *measures*, which are separated by *bar lines*. In all of the exercises below, there are four beats in each measure. A *double bar* shows the end of the exercise.

Try these exercises.
Practice whispering "tu" on each note (not playing the recorder yet).

♩ = *Quarter note.* One beat (count).

1
Track 1

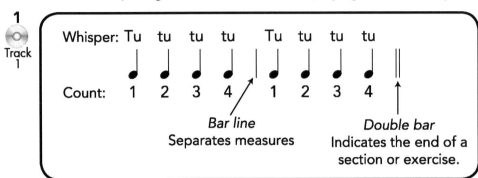

Now clap once for each note and count aloud ("1-2-3-4"), trying to keep the beat as steady as a ticking clock.

2
Track 2

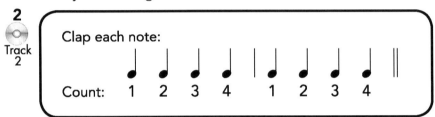

In the next exercise, tongue ("tu") and play the quarter-note Bs on your recorder.

3
Track 3

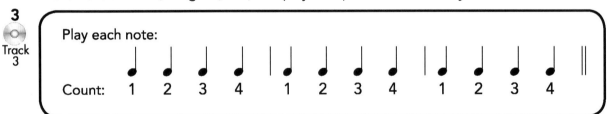

Try counting aloud and clapping the next pattern of notes and rests (the rhythm), holding your hands apart for the rests. A rest is a symbol that indicates silence. Each quarter rest receives one beat, same as each quarter note. Say: "1-2-3-rest, 1-2-3-rest, 1-2-3-rest, 1-2-3-rest."

4
Track 4

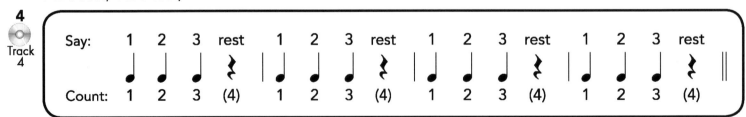

Practice this exercise two different ways:
1. Finger the note while you name it and the rests, saying "B-B-B-rest," etc.
2. Play it on the recorder.

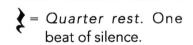
= *Quarter rest.* One beat of silence.

5
Track 5

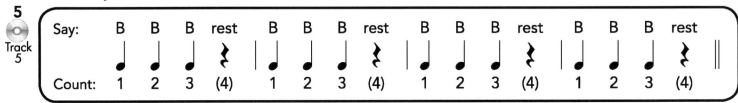

The Staff and the Musical Alphabet

In Chapter 2, you will learn some new notes and begin playing exercises that combine different notes. This page covers the basic information that you will need to begin reading music.

Notes are written on a *staff* which is a group of five lines and four spaces.

As you know, bar lines separate groups of beats called measures. A *G clef* (also called *treble clef*) appears at the beginning of each staff. A clef tells us which lines and spaces represent which notes. The G clef encircles the G line. Any note placed on that line is called G.

At the beginning of each piece there is a *time signature*. The top number in a time signature tells how many beats there are in each measure, and the bottom number tells us what kind of note gets one beat. ¼ means that there are four beats per measure and a quarter note gets one beat.

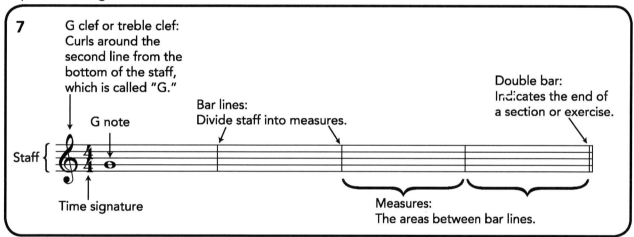

Staff lines and spaces are numbered like this:

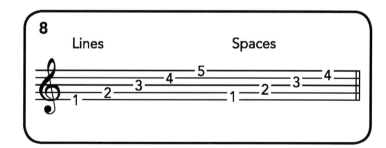

The musical alphabet uses only seven letters to the name the pitches (musical sounds). The seven letter names repeat. The pitches ascend as we go forward through the alphabet and descend as we go backwards.

The higher a note is placed on the staff, the higher it sounds. Here are the names of the notes on the staff. Don't bother trying to memorize them all now, just notice how the note names go forward through the alphabet as they ascend the staff.

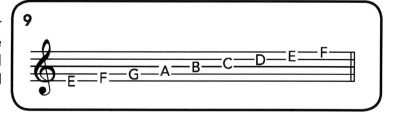

Things to Remember

In $\frac{4}{4}$ time:

- There are four beats in each measure.
- A quarter note (♩ or ♪) gets one beat. Notes lower than B (the middle staff line) have their stems going up on the right.
- A quarter rest ❜ indicates one beat of silence.

Introducing B

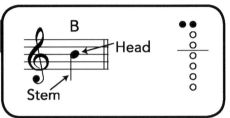

Here is the note B on the staff. It is on the third line. Notice that the note has two parts: the *head* and the *stem*.

Play these exercises.

11
Track
6.2
Count: 1 (2) 3 (4) 1 2 3 (4) 1 (2) 3 (4) (1) 2 3 (4)

Introducing A

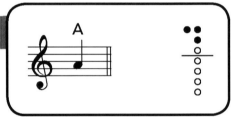

The note A is written one place lower on the staff than B, on the second space. Add a finger to the next hole down to create this lower- sounding pitch.

Second-Space A

12
Track
7.1
Count: 1 2 3 4 1 (2) 3 (4) 1 2 3 4 1 2 3 (4)

Bs and As

13
Track
7.2
Count: 1 (2) 3 (4) 1 2 3 4 1 2 3 (4) 1 (2) 3 (4)

Faster Bs and As

Try to finger and name the notes aloud before playing this one.

14
Track
7.3
Count: 1 2 3 4 1 2 3 4 (1) 2 3 4 (1) 2 3 4

Introducing G

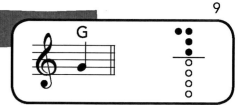

G is written on the second line of the staff. To play a G, add a finger to the 3rd hole. You should have your left-hand thumb, 1st, 2nd and 3rd fingers covering holes.

Second-Line G

 15 Track 8.1

Count: 1 2 (3) 4 1 (2) 3 (4) 1 2 3 (4) 1 (2) 3 (4)

A Mixed "BAG"

16 Track 8.2

Count: 1 2 3 4 1 2 3 (4) 1 2 3 4 1 2 3 (4)

The Half Note and Half Rest

♩ 𝅗𝅥 = *Half note.* Lasts twice as long as a quarter note. It gets two beats.

▬ = *Half rest.* Indicates two beats of silence.

' = *Breathmark.* Tells you to take a quick, quiet breath, taking your top lip off the recorder. Rests are good places to breathe, too.

Play this example that uses half notes, quarter notes and a half rest.

17 Track 9.1

Count: 1 2 3 4 1 2 3 4 1 2 3 4 1 2 (3) (4)

In the next exercise, there are two places you have to move two fingers at the same time to change from B to G.

18 Track 9.2

Count: 1 2 3 4 1 2 (3) (4) 1 2 3 4 1 2 3 (4)

Notice the *final double bar* at the end of this piece. This is used to show the end of a piece of music.

Hot Cross Buns
Track 10

Traditional

Count: 1 2 3 4 1 2 (3) (4) 1 2 3 4 1 2 (3) (4) 1 2 3 4 1 2 3 4 1 2 3 4 1 2 (3) (4)

Final double bar

Now try to play *Hot Cross Buns* from memory. See if you can feel your fingers covering the holes without looking down at them.

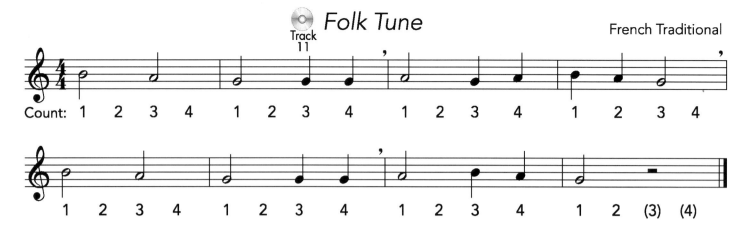

Folk Tune

French Traditional

Count: 1 2 3 4   1 2 3 4   1 2 3 4   1 2 3 4

1 2 3 4   1 2 3 4   1 2 3 4   1 2 (3) (4)

This next piece is a *duet*. A duet is a piece for two musicians playing different parts at the same time. The result, the sound of two notes being played together, is called *harmony*. Harmony can be even more beautiful than a single melody. Play this with your teacher, a friend or the CD that is available for this book. You could also record yourself playing one of the parts and then play along with the recording. When you repeat it, try trading parts.

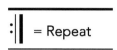

= Repeat

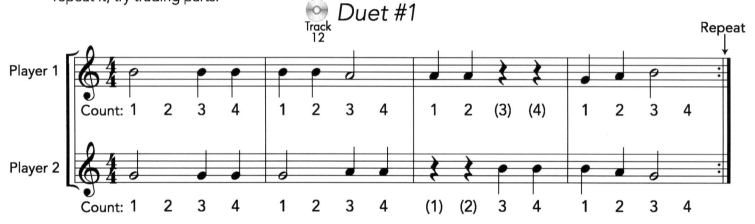

Duet #1

Repeat

Player 1

Count: 1 2 3 4   1 2 3 4   1 2 (3) (4)   1 2 3 4

Player 2

Count: 1 2 3 4   1 2 3 4   (1) (2) 3 4   1 2 3 4

A *Bransle* is a dance from the Renaissance period (roughly 1450–1600).

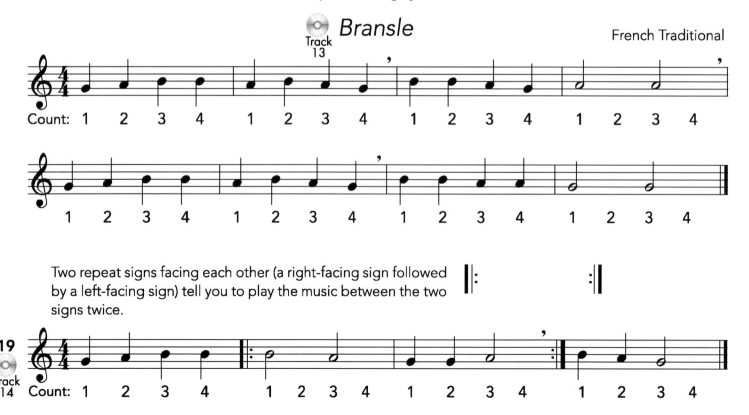

Bransle

French Traditional

Count: 1 2 3 4   1 2 3 4   1 2 3 4   1 2 3 4

1 2 3 4   1 2 3 4   1 2 3 4   1 2 3 4

Two repeat signs facing each other (a right-facing sign followed by a left-facing sign) tell you to play the music between the two signs twice.

19

Count: 1 2 3 4   1 2 3 4   1 2 3 4   1 2 3 4

The Whole Note and Whole Rest

o = *Whole note.* Is twice as long as a half note and gets four beats.

▬ = *Whole rest.* Indicates four beats of silence.

You can think of the whole rest as "hanging down" because four beats are "heavier" than two are.

Comparing Whole Rests and Half Rests

Notice the difference:

Half rest sits on third line.

20

Whole rest hangs from fourth line.

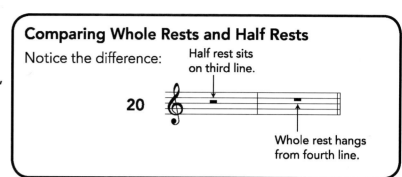

Frog in the Meadow

North Carolina
Game Song

Mary's Lamb

Traditional

In French, *Pierrot* (pronounced Pyair-o) means "little Peter."

Pierrot

French Traditional

Try clapping each part of *Duet #2* before playing. Notice the rests! Also notice that the rhythm (pattern of note and rest values) is different in the two parts.

Duet #2

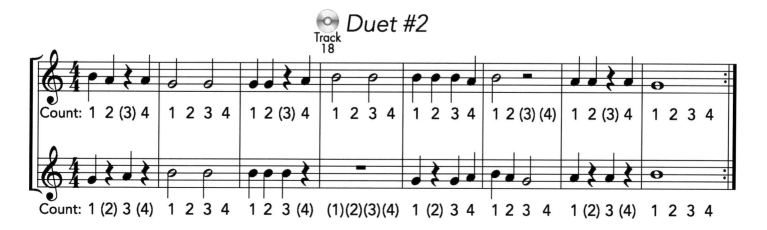

Chapter 2

More Notes & Rhythm Concepts

Introducing C

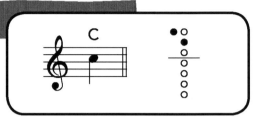

The note C is written on the third space of the staff. Find the note C on the recorder by playing A and then lifting the 1st finger off the 1st hole so that only your thumb and 2nd finger are covering holes.

C–A, C–G, C–B Study

The C–B finger change is probably the most difficult because there is a direct alternation of the 1st and 2nd fingers. Practice slowly at first.

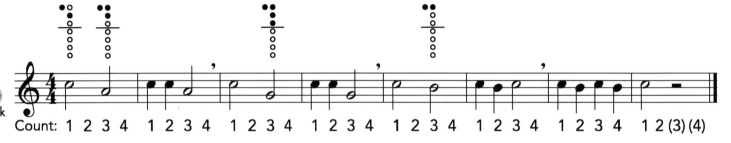

21 Track 19 Count: 1 2 3 4   1 2 3 4   1 2 3 4   1 2 3 4   1 2 3 4   1 2 3 4   1 2 3 4   1 2 (3) (4)

A *rigaudon* (pronounced ree-goh-DOHN) is another Renaissance dance. The great English composer Henry Purcell (1659–1695) enjoyed composing in French dance forms, as did composers all over Europe in the late 17th and early 18th centuries.

Rigaudon
Track 20

Henry Purcell

Count: 1   2   3   4   1   2   3   4   1   2   3   4   1   2   3   4

1   2   3   4   1   2   3   4   1   2   3   4   1   2   3   4

Notice how many times the notes of the first two measures of this piece repeat.

Juba
Track 21

American Traditional

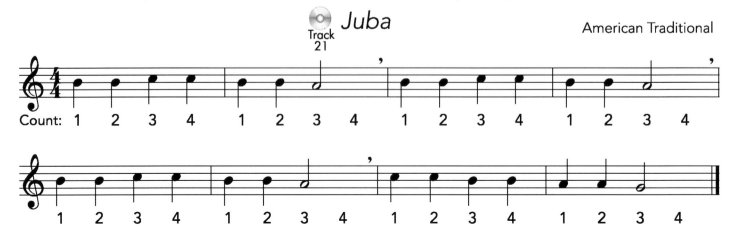

Count: 1   2   3   4   1   2   3   4   1   2   3   4   1   2   3   4

1   2   3   4   1   2   3   4   1   2   3   4   1   2   3   4

Try adding the bar lines in the next exercise. Watch for half rests and whole rests. The correct answers are shown at the bottom of page 20. Clapping the exercise as you count aloud will give you a feeling for the rhythm. Try clapping it backwards, too (reading from right to left). The resulting rhythm will be entirely different.

22

Introducing $\frac{2}{4}$ Time

In $\frac{2}{4}$ time, there are two beats in each measure and the quarter note gets one beat.

> **2** = Two beats per measure
> **4** = Quarter note ♩ gets one beat

Chanson is the French word for "song." Notice the numbers over some of the bar lines. These are "rehearsal numbers" or "measure numbers." They provide points of reference and help simplify communication between musicians. For example, it's a good idea to practice measures 5 and 6 of *Chanson* out of context before playing the whole piece. There, you see? Having those measure numbers in the music are a big help.

Chanson

Track 22

French

Count: 1 2 1 2 1 2 1 2 1 2 1 2 1 2 1 2

1 2 1 2 1 2 1 2 1 2 1 2 1 2 1 2

Think where breathmarks might go in *Russian Folk Tune*. Maybe you can play it without marking them.

Russian Folk Tune

Track 23

Traditional

Count: 1 2 1 2 1 2 1 2 1 2 1 2 1 2 1 2

1 2 1 2 1 2 1 2 1 2 1 2 1 2 1 2

Sound Check (for tone quality):
- While you're trying hard to play the right notes and rhythms, try not to blow harder.
- Think of blowing a slow breath, as if you're warming your hands on a cold day.
- Remember to "tu" each note, but keep a steady stream of air coming for a smoother sound. To see if your air is steady, play four Bs, then four As in a row. Listen for connected notes without spaces in between.

Introducing D

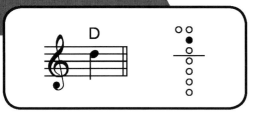

D is written on the fourth line of the staff. To find the D on the recorder, play a C and then lift the thumb off its hole. Make sure your right-hand thumb is helping to support the recorder, or you'll drop it! Also, keep your left thumb near the recorder, just behind its hole.

Linking Up to D in Steps and Skips

Steps are the distances between notes that are neighbors on the staff (space to line or line to space), and in the musical alphabet (A to B is a step; B to C is a step; and G to F is a step). *Skips* are the distances between notes that are not direct neighbors but jump up or down, skipping one or more notes in the musical alphabet (A to C and A to D are skips).

Go Tell Aunt Rhody

American Traditional

Duet #3—Lady, Come

English Traditional

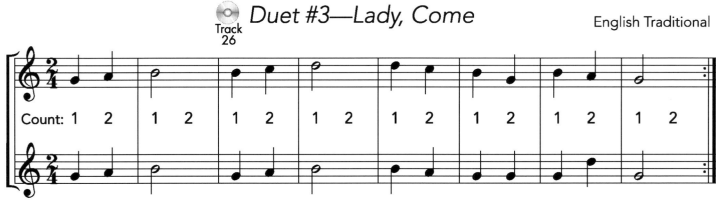

Ties

A *tie* is a curved line that joins two or more notes of the same pitch. Only the first note is played, lasting the duration of their combined note values. For example, a half note (two beats) tied to a quarter note (one beat) lasts three beats.

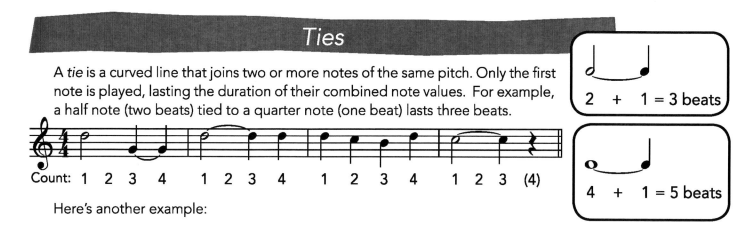

Count: 1 2 3 4   1 2 3 4   1 2 3 4   1 2 3 (4)

Here's another example:

A whole note (four beats) tied to a quarter note (one beat) lasts five beats.

Track 27
When the Saints Go Marching In
Traditional

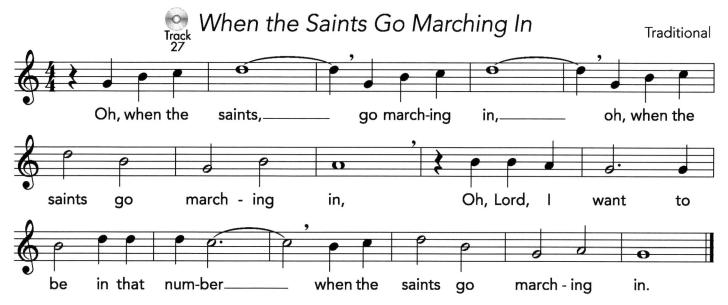

Oh, when the saints,_____ go march-ing in,_____ oh, when the
saints go march - ing in, Oh, Lord, I want to
be in that num-ber_____ when the saints go march - ing in.

Dots

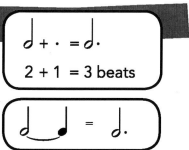

A *dot* to the right of a note increases the note's value by one half. For example, a half note equals two beats. Half of that value is one beat. So, a *dotted half note* lasts three beats (2+1=3).

You can also think of a dotted half note as being equal to a half note tied to a quarter note.

The same is true of a *dotted half rest*: A half rest indicates two beats of silence. Half of that value is one beat of silence (a quarter rest). So, a dotted half rest indicates three beats of silence. ▬· Dotted half rests are rarely used.

Aura Lee is an American folk song that Elvis Presley used as the melody for his hit song, *Love Me Tender*. Here is part of the melody from that song.

Track 28
Aura Lee
American Folk Song

Count: 1 2 3 4 1 2 3 4 1 2 3 4 1 2 3 4 1 2 3 4 1 2 3 4 1 2 3 4 1 2 3 (4)

Introducing ¾ Time

In ¾ time, there are three beats in every measure. Since the bottom number is 4, the quarter note gets one beat, as in ¼ time and ¼ time. ¾ is sometimes referred to as *waltz* time because the dance called the *waltz*, which originated in the 18th century, is in ¾.

> **3** = Three beats per measure
> **4** = Quarter note ♩ gets one beat

The Nightingale

Track 29

French Traditional

A *barcarolle* is music in the style of songs sung by Venetian gondoliers. The following tune is from the opera *Tales of Hoffman*, by the composer Jacques Offenbach (1819–1880), who was famous for his operas and ballets.

Barcarolle

Track 30

Jacques Offenbach

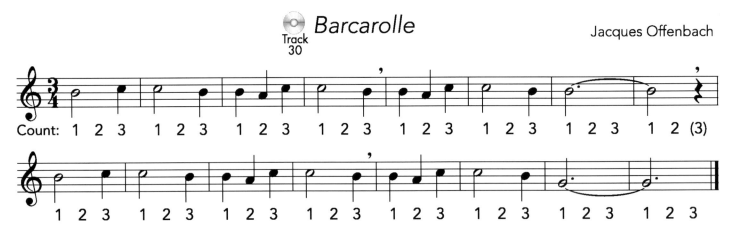

Try clapping this next piece before playing it, saying "short" for the quarter notes and "long" for the half notes ♩. Say "long, 2, 3" for the dotted half notes.

The Cuckoo

Track 31

German Traditional

Pickup Notes

Not all pieces start on the first beat of the measure. The note (or notes) before the first complete measure are called *pickup notes*. Here are two examples of pickups:

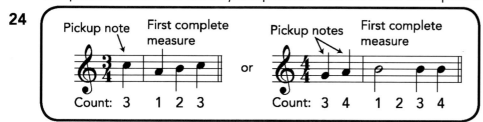

Notice that the beats needed to complete the pickup measure are found in the last measure. This is called an *incomplete measure*.

Folk Song
German Traditional

Composition Exercise #1

Composition is the act of writing original music. Even if you don't plan to be a composer, trying your hand at some composition will give you a deeper understanding of music. Also, it's fun!

As a composer, you can try adding four measures of your own to those given below. Here are some tips:

- Make sure there are four beats (no more, no less) in each measure.
- Write neatly so you can read and play it.
- If the completed composition suggests a mood or a scene, give it a name (or, call it *Opus #1*, meaning your "first work").
- Use a pencil instead of a pen so that you can correct errors easily or in case you change you mind. Notice the direction and placement of the note stems.

For notes A and lower, stems go up on the right. For notes B and higher, stems go down on the left.

Here are the first four measures of your first composition. Fill in the blank measures to finish the piece. Enjoy!

Chapter 3

Low Notes, Sharps, Flats & Articulations

Introducing Low E

Low E is written on the first line of the staff. To play E, finger a G with the left hand and then add the 1st and 2nd right-hand fingers. Check your right thumb position. Keeping the thumb just behind the right-hand 1st finger will help you find the correct holes.

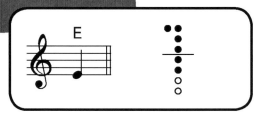

Track 33 — Chinese Folk Tune

Traditional

Count: 1 2 3 4   1 2 3 4   1 2 3 4   1 2 3 4   1 2 3 4   1 2 3 4

Hills and Dales uses only notes on the lines of the staff. See if you can still finger and name the notes in rhythm (without hesitating) before playing.

Track 34 — Hills and Dales

Count: 1 2 3   1 2 3   1 2 3   1 2 (3)   1 2 3   1 2 3   1 2 3   1 2 3

Note Review—Musical Word Games

The letter names of these notes spell words. Write the letter names in the spaces provided to see what words they spell. The correct answers for these examples are on the bottom of page 27.

27

Now, write the notes for the words below:

28

D E E D   A D D   B E A D E D   B A D G E

Whole Steps and Half Steps

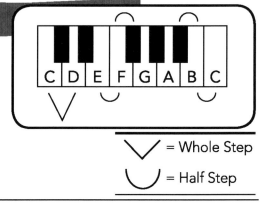

= Whole Step

= Half Step

As you know, the musical alphabet is as follows: A-B-C-D-E-F-G-A-B-C, etc. Adjacent notes in the musical alphabet, such as A and B or F and G, are said to be a *step* apart. There are two kinds of steps: *whole steps* and *half steps*. Think of a piano keyboard (on the right). Notes with black keys between them are *whole steps*. The distance from a white key to an adjacent black is a *half step*. Notice that E to F and B to C are also half steps.

Introducing the Sharp ♯

Accidentals are symbols that change the pitch of a note. The sharp sign ♯ raises the note one half step. The F♯ (say "F sharp") lies between the notes F and G. On the piano keyboard, it is a black key between two white keys. If the F is repeated in the same measure, it is automatically still sharped. The sharp sign is not repeated (see *Polish Folk Song* below).

Introducing Low F♯

To play F♯, finger a G with the left hand and then add the 2nd and 3rd fingers of the right hand.

After repeating the first line of *Renaissance Dance*, proceed to the second.

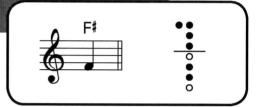

While practicing the next exercise, think of keeping the right-hand middle finger down while the 1st and 3rd fingers move. Play *slowly* until it becomes easy for you.

20

Key Signatures

A *key signature* is an accidental or a group of accidentals at the beginning of a staff. When there is an F♯ in the key signature, as in the next three pieces, all Fs, low and high, are to be played as F♯.

Nöel is a Christmas song by the French composer Nicolas Chedeville (1705–1782). Be sure to play all the Fs as F♯s.

Notice the *legato* marking at the beginning of the next piece, *French Folk Song*. Legato is the term used to indicate a smooth playing style with no spaces between notes except for at breaths.

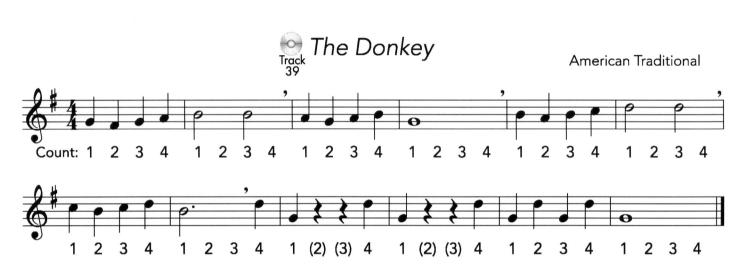

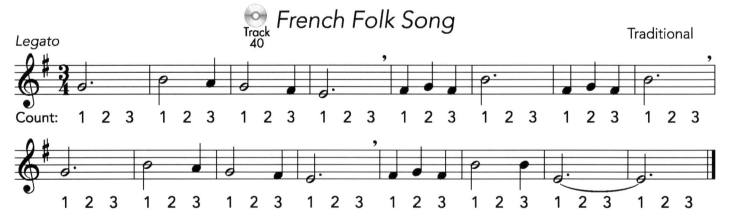

Answers to Example 22, page 13.

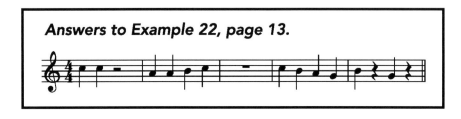

Introducing Low D

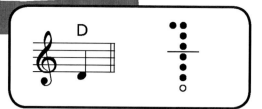

Low D is written in the space immediately below the staff. To play low D, finger a low E (page 18) and add the right-hand 3rd finger. It may take some practice to seal all the holes, especially this new double hole.

The Low D Connections

In *Scotland's Burning*, notice the use of both high and low Ds. This piece can also be played as a round (the same melody played together starting at two different times). When player #1 gets to the third measure, (marked with an asterisk [*]), player #2 starts at the beginning. Now it's a duet.

Scotland's Burning

This traditional Christmas song, written by Benjamin Hanby in the 1870s, is presented here as a duet. Note the key signature. Have fun!

Jolly Old Saint Nicholas

Eighth Notes and Eighth Rests

An eighth note lasts half as long as a quarter note. If you tap your foot along with a piece of music, you will notice that there are two parts to every beat: the part where your foot is down on the ground and the part where it is up in the air. Each of those parts is half a beat in duration. As long as a quarter note gets one beat, an eighth note will equal half of a beat.

Clap and count aloud these examples:

$\flat$ = A single eighth note gets half a beat.

γ = An eighth rest indicates half a beat of silence.

Consecutive eighth notes are beamed together.

To count eighth notes, divide the beat into two, calling the second part "&" ("and").

31
Track 44.1
Count: 1 & 2 (&) 1 & 2 &

32
Track 44.2
Count: 1 & 2 & 1 & 2 & 1 & 2 & 1 & (2) (&)

Jingle Bells Duet
Track 45

James Pierpont (1857)
Arr. S. Lowenkron

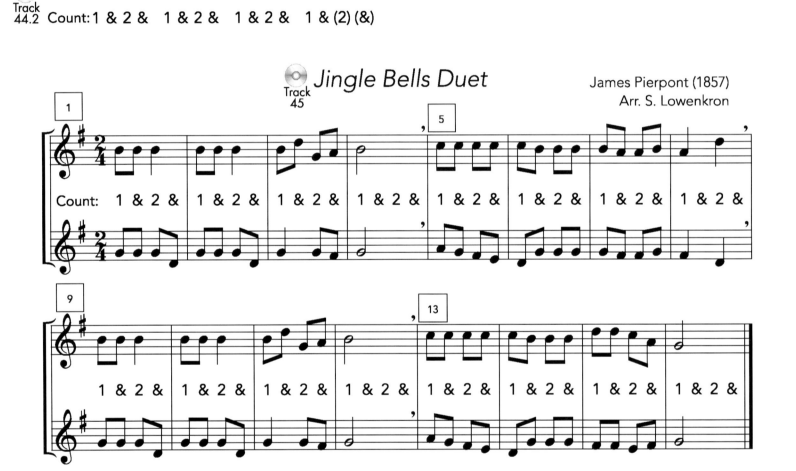

Count: 1 & 2 & | 1 & 2 & | 1 & 2 & | 1 & 2 & | 1 & 2 & | 1 & 2 & | 1 & 2 & | 1 & 2 &

1 & 2 & | 1 & 2 & | 1 & 2 & | 1 & 2 & | 1 & 2 & | 1 & 2 & | 1 & 2 & | 1 & 2 &

Practicing the Eighth Rest
It's a good idea to clap and count aloud before playing.

33
Track 46

Count: 1 (&) 2 (&) 1 & 2 & 1 & 2 (&) 1 & 2 & 1 & 2 & 1 (&) 2 (&) 1 & 2 & 1 (&) 2 &

Musette is the French word for "bagpipes." A piece with this title usually has a drone in the bass line. The following is a melody from a musette by Bach.

Musette

J. S. Bach

Track 47

Count: 1   2   3 & 4 &   1   2   3 & 4 &   1 & 2   3   4   1   2   3   4

1   2   3 & 4 &   1   2   3 & 4 &   1 & 2   3   4   1   2   3   4

Introducing Low F

To play the note F, put all the fingers down except for the middle finger of the right hand. You may have to adjust the foot joint of the recorder (see page 4) so your pinky can completely cover the bottom double hole.

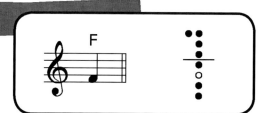

The G–F, E–F and D–F Connections

34

Track 48

Count: 1 2 3 4   1 2 3 4   1 2 3 4   1 & 2 (3) 4   1 2 3 & 4   1 & 2 & 3 4   1 2 3 (4)

Use the rests as opportunities to breathe.

The Carnival of Venice

J. Bellack

Track 49

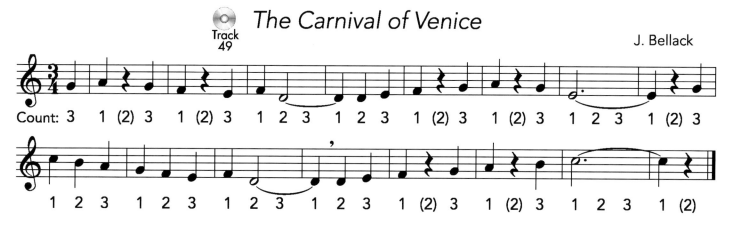

Count: 3   1 (2) 3   1 (2) 3   1 2 3   1 2 3   1 (2) 3   1 (2) 3   1 2 3   1 (2) 3

1 2 3   1 2 3   1 2 3   1 2 3   1 (2) 3   1 (2) 3   1 2 3   1 (2)

Shortnin' Bread

American Traditional
(Southern)

Track 50

Count: 1   2 & 3   4   1 & 2   3   4   1   2   3   4 &   1 & 2   3 (4)   1   2 & 3   4   1   2   3   4

1   2   3 & 4   1   2   3 (4)   1 & 2 & 3 & 4   1   2   3   4   1 & 2 & 3 & 4   1   2   3 (4)

The Dotted Quarter Note

As you know, a dot to the right of a note increases its value by one half. A dotted half note, for example, gets three beats (page 15). Since a quarter note equals one beat, and half of that value is half a beat, a dotted quarter note equals one-and-a-half beats. You can also think of a dotted quarter note as being equal to a quarter note tied to an eighth note.

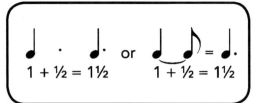

Look at example 35. You will see that measures 2 and 3 have the same rhythm, but with different note values. Clap this new rhythm as you count aloud. Notice that the dotted quarter note takes the time of three eighth notes ("1-&, 2").

35

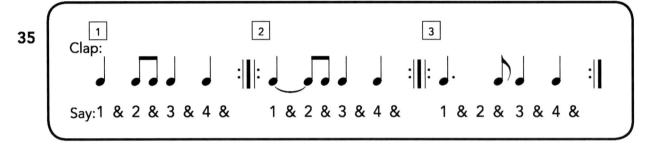

Example 36 also shows two ways of writing the same rhythm.

36

In $\frac{2}{4}$, $\frac{3}{4}$, and $\frac{4}{4}$, the dotted quarter note is often followed by a single eighth note, which creates a two-beat figure:

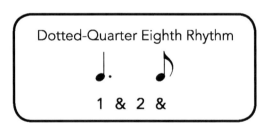

Piano Sonata Theme

Track 51

W. A. Mozart

Notice the key signature in the next pieces.

Articulations

Articulation is the manner in which a note is played. You learned legato on page 20, which is an articulation style that means to play smooth and connected (no spaces between the notes). Here are two more types of articulation:

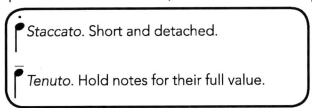

Introducing Low C

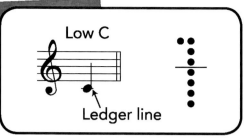

Low C on the recorder is the same pitch that is called *middle* C on other instruments. Low C is written on the first *ledger* line below the staff. A ledger line is a short horizontal line used to extend the staff either higher or lower.

Here are some tips for playing low C:

- C is the lowest tone you can play on the soprano recorder, and it is a quiet note.
- It is important to blow very gently and hold fingers down firmly ("blow light, hold tight").
- If your recorder has a moveable foot joint, it will help to adjust it so the pinky can reach it more easily (without a big stretch).
- When going for the C, be careful that the double holes for D are also well covered.
- If the tone is unclear or squeaky, try clearing the windway (see page 4). Too much moisture often affects the lowest notes on the recorder.

It is easy to approach C from F first because only one finger is added.

Approach C from F

Then, approach it stepwise on long tones.

Approach C Step by Step

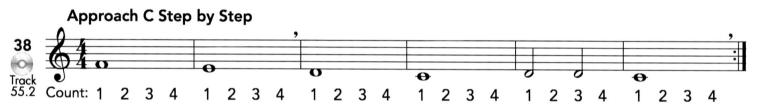

Here's an exercise using larger skips.

Octaves

You now know two Ds (low and high) and two Cs (low and high). Because the distance between the two Ds and the two Cs is eight notes, they are called *octaves* (related to words like "octagon" and "octopus"). You'll see octaves in the next piece.

My Bonny Lad

Scottish Traditional

We Gather Together (Hymn)

17th-Century Dutch

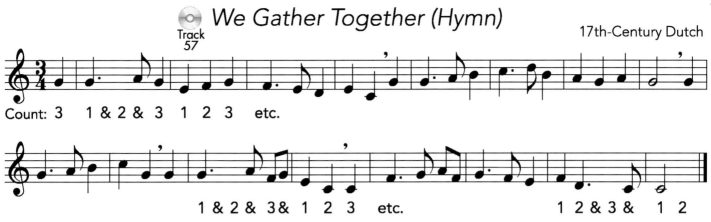

Count: 3 1 & 2 & 3 1 2 3 etc.

1 & 2 & 3& 1 2 3 etc.   1 2 & 3 & 1 2

Kookaburra is a two-part round. The second player enters at measure 3 (marked *).

Kookaburra

Australian Traditional

Count: 1 & 2 & 3 4 & 1 2 3 4 etc.

1 2 3 & 4 & etc.   1 2 3 (4)

Rigaudon

Jacques Hotteterre

Count: 4 1 2 3 4 1 2 & 3 4 etc.   1 2 3

Composition Exercise #2

Using the dotted-quarter-and-eighth-note figure (and a Low C or two), try your hand at expanding these two measures into a four-measure piece:

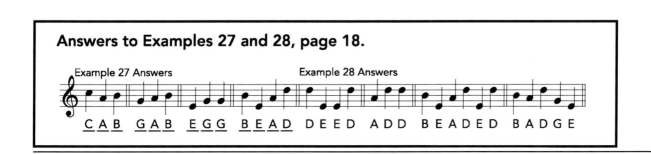

Answers to Examples 27 and 28, page 18.

Example 27 Answers   Example 28 Answers

CAB GAB EGG BEAD DEED ADD BEADED BADGE

Introducing the Flat ♭

The *flat* sign ♭ lowers a note by one half step. The B♭ (say "B flat") lies between the notes A and B. On the piano keyboard, it is a black key between two white keys. If the B is repeated in the same measure, it is automatically still flatted. The flat sign is not repeated. In a piece where we want all the Bs flatted, we can use the B♭ in the key signature.

Introducing B♭

B♭ is played with the left-hand thumb, 1st and 3rd fingers and the right-hand 1st finger.

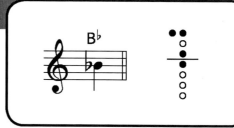

The B♭ Connections
B♭ is an easy note to play but somewhat difficult to connect to other notes. Practice slowly at first. Notice the key signature. All Bs are flatted.

41
Track
60

Lovely Evening is a round, like *Scotland's Burnin'* on page 21. The second player comes in at measure 7 (marked with an asterisk *). The third player enters at measure 13.

Lovely Evening (Round)
Track
61

German Traditional

The Streets of Laredo
Track
62

American Traditional

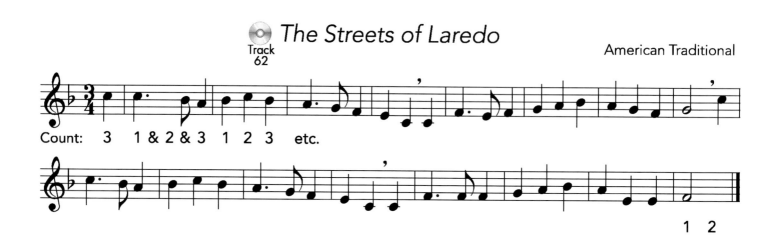

Count:　3　1 & 2 & 3　1　2　3　etc.

1　2

Chapter 4

Scales & Dynamics

The Major Scale

A scale is a group of notes that follow a specific pattern of whole steps (W) and half steps (H). There are many kinds of scales and perhaps the most important scale is the major scale. It has a specific arrangement of whole steps and half steps that is always the same, no matter on which note you start. The pattern for the major scale is:

Notice in the diagram below that each note in the scale is given a number, and that half steps occur between 3 & 4 and 7 & 8.

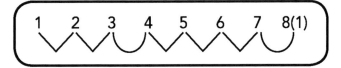

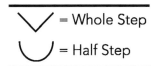

The C Major Scale

42
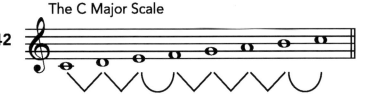

The F Major Scale

43
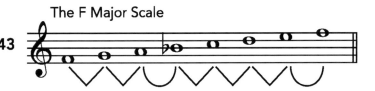

The first note of a major scale is called the *tonic*. All notes that result from building a major scale on a particular tonic are the notes that make up that particular key. For example, the notes following this whole-step/half-step pattern starting on G (G A B C D E F♯ G) comprise the key of G.

It is because of this pattern for major scales that the B♭ occurs in the key of F, and the F♯ occurs in the key of G.

Now that you know what scales look like, you'll recognize parts of them, or even entire scales, in many of the pieces you play. Below are two *scalar* (made with scales) pieces. *Lavender's Blue* is in F and *Can Can* is in C.

Lavender's Blue

Track 63

Traditional

Count: 1 2 3 1 2 & 3 & 1 2 3 1 2 3 etc.

This piece includes a completely unchanged descending C Major scale.

Can-Can

Track 64

Jacques Offenbach

C Major Scale

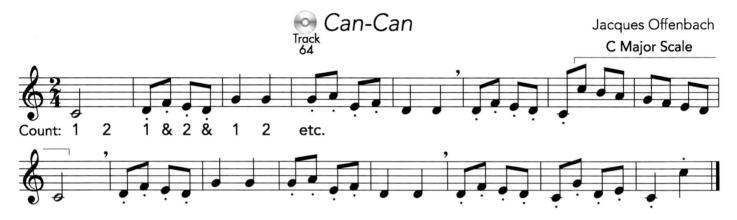

Count: 1 2 1 & 2 & 1 2 etc.

The Slur

Like the staccato and the tenuto marks, the *slur* is an articulation. It is a curved line above or below the note heads that connects two or more notes of different pitches. When notes are slurred, only the first note of the group is tongued ("tu") to create a legato sound.

44 Track 65.1

Tongue: Tu Tu Tu tu Tu tu tu

45 Track 65.2

Tu Tu Tu tu Tu

Here's the C Major scale in two different slurring patterns:

46 Track 65.3

47 Track 65.4

Now go back to *Lavender's Blue*, playing the eighth notes in two-note slurs, like this:

48

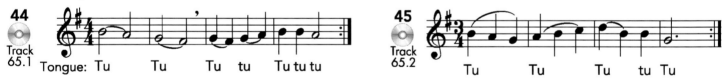
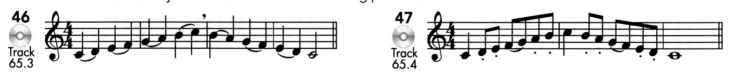

Accents

The *accent* sign > above or below a note head means to make that note louder than the surrounding notes. This is another way of bringing out musical expression in a piece. Blow an accelerated burst of air, but tongue a "du" rather than a "tu." Otherwise, you may "crack" or "split" the sound.

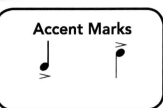

Accent Marks

Here is an example using accents:

Tongue: Du · · du Du · du

Syncopation

In *syncopation*, accents are shifted from the strong beats (or strong parts of the beats) to the weak beats (or weak parts of the beats). In $\frac{4}{4}$, beat 1, the downbeat, is the strongest beat, and beat 3 is considered somewhat strong, as well. Beats 2 and 4 are the weaker beats. The second half of a beat, the "&," sometimes called the "off-beat" or the "up-beat," is the weak part of a beat. Playing on the weak beats, or especially the off-beats, gives music a jazzy, "up-tempo" feel.

Below are three syncopated exercises to learn. Make sure you count and clap them first.

Count: (1) 2 (3) 4 (1) 2 (3) 4 1 2 (3) 4 1 2 3 (4)

(1) & 2 & (1) & (2) & (1) & 2 & 1 2

These measures are written differently, but sound the same.

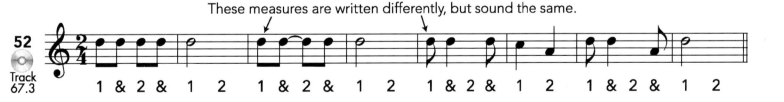

1 & 2 & 1 2 1 & 2 & 1 2 1 & 2 & 1 2 1 & 2 & 1 2

Liza Jane

Track 68

American Traditional

1 & 2 & 1 & 2 &

A *dreydl* (pronounced ("dray-del") is a spinning top associated with Hanukkah,
a Jewish holiday.

Dreydl

Track 69

Hanukkah Song

Count: &   1 & 2 &   1 & 2 &   1 & 2 &   1 & 2 &   etc.

1 & 2

Shule Aroon

Track 70

Irish Air

Legato

Count: 4   1   2   3   4   1 & 2 & 3 & 4 &   1 & 2 & 3 & 4 &   1 & 2 & 3 & 4 &

etc.

1   2   3

In ¾ time, beat 1 is the only strong beat; beats 2 and 3 are weak. In *Quem Pastores*, a
song which first appeared in 1555, syncopation is created by a long, stressed note on
beat 2.

Quem Pastores

Track 71

Early Christmas Carol

Dynamics

Dynamics are the loudness and softness of music. Dynamic markings are used to communicate different volume levels. Though there are many levels of volume, the two most basic markings are as follows:

> f = *Forte* (fohr-teh). Loud
> p = *Piano* (pyah-noh). Soft

These are Italian words (like most other musical expressions).

Dynamics, especially in pre-19th century music, are often not marked in the music so the performer can choose them. On the recorder, it is easy to "crack" a note if played too loudly. A little trick to make dynamic differences stand out on this instrument is as follows:

1. Play louder (forte) passages of music more connected (legato).
2. Play softer (piano) passages more detached (a gentle staccato).

$\mathbf{C}$ = A time signature that stands for *common time*. Common time is another way of expressing $\frac{4}{4}$.

O! No John

Track 72

English Traditional

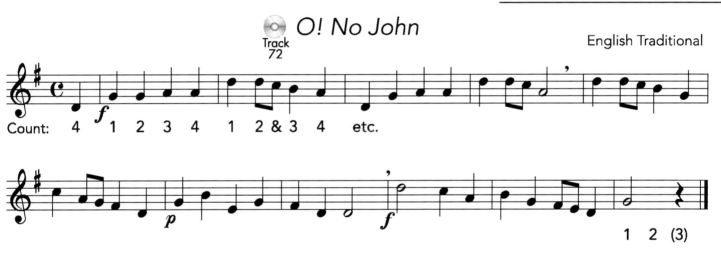

Count: 4   1 2 3 4   1   2 & 3   4   etc.

1   2 (3)

$\frown$ = *Fermata* (sometimes called a "hold" or "bird's eye"). It means to hold the note slightly longer than written.

How Beautifully Shines the Morning Star

Track 73

German Traditional

Count: 4   1 2 3 4   etc.

1   2   3

Chapter 5

High Notes, ⅜ Time & More

Introducing High E

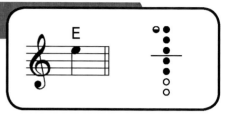

High E is written in the fourth space. The fingering for high E is the same as for low E, except a small part of your thumbhole is uncovered. Here are two methods for doing this:

1) Bend your thumb at the top joint and pinch your thumbnail into the hole, leaving only a small part of the thumbhole open above the thumbnail.

2) Bend your thumb and pinch the thumbhole with only the fleshy part of your thumb.

You may have to experiment to see which method gets the clearest tone. Either way, you'll notice that you have to blow a little more (speed up your air).

High E Connections

Mother Says Go On Dear Children

American (Shaker)

This is another song that makes a good round. The second player can enter at measure 5 (at the asterisk *).

Hey! Ho! Nobody Home

Old English

Introducing High F

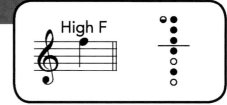

High F is written on the fifth (top) line of the staff. The fingering for high F is the same as for low F except:

1) The bottom double-hole is left uncovered by the right pinky.

2) You need to "pinch" ("crack" open) the left thumb as for high E (and all higher notes).

High F Connections
Remember that all Bs are flatted.

54 Track 77

Yankee Doodle
Track 78

American Traditional

Now that you know both low and high F, you can play the F Major scale.

F Major Scale

55

1st and 2nd Endings
When a piece is repeated, we often need to play something different at the end of the second time through. This is often written with *1st* and *2nd endings*. We play through to the first repeat sign in the 1st ending, and then repeat. When we arrive at the 1st ending on the repeat, we skip it and play the 2nd ending instead.

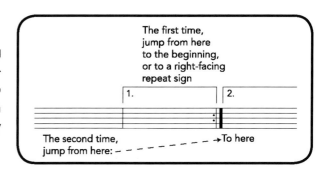

The first time, jump from here to the beginning, or to a right-facing repeat sign

1.   2.

The second time, jump from here: → To here

Duet: Theme from The New World Symphony
Track 79

Antonin Dvořák

Introducing High C#

This is another "no-thumb" fingering, like the D you learned on page 14. Think of A (page 8) and take off the thumb.

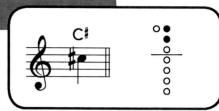

Now that you know the note C#, you can build another scale, this time starting on D.

The D Major Scale
Note the new key signature; all Fs and Cs are sharped.

New Key Signature: D Major

56

Joy to the World
Track 80

G. F. Handel

Introducing The Natural ♮

A *natural sign* ♮ cancels a sharp or a flat. It will cancel a sharp or flat in a key signature or an accidental that occured earlier in the measure for the duration of the measure in which it appears.

Here's a challenging excerpt from a well-known piano piece. Keep an eye out for accidentals.

Für Elise
Track 81

Ludwig van Beethoven

D.C and D.S. Signs

D.C. al Fine (pronounced Da Capo al FEE-neh) tells you to go back to the beginning and play until the Fine.

An *Allemande* is a German dance. Composers of all nationalities often used it in *suites*. Suites were collections of short pieces, most of which were dances.

Allemande

Track 82

Claude Gervaise

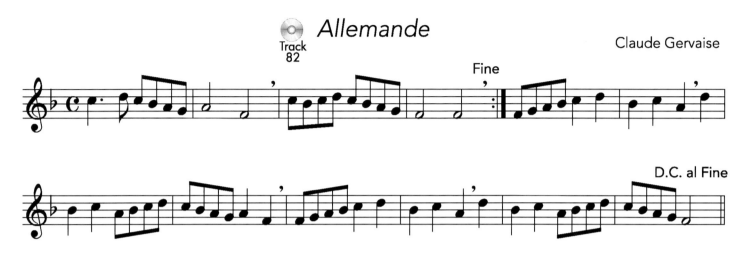

D.S. al Fine (Dal Segno, pronounced SAY-nyo) tells you to go back to the sign 𝄋 and play until the Fine.

There are some dynamics (*f* and *p*), ties and a fermata 𝄐 in this tune, also.

For He's a Jolly Good Fellow

Track 83

Traditional

⁶⁄₈ Time

⁶⁄₈ is a time signature in which the eighth note gets one beat. Until now, all of the time signatures you have learned have had a **4** on the bottom, indicating that the quarter note gets one beat. In ⁶⁄₈, things are different:

> **6** = Six beats per measure
> **8** = The eighth note ♪ gets one beat

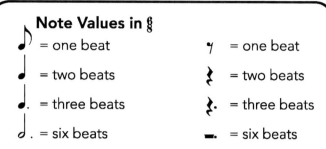

Note Values in ⁶⁄₈

♪ = one beat	⁊ = one beat
♩ = two beats	𝄽 = two beats
♩. = three beats	𝄽. = three beats
♪. = six beats	▬. = six beats

The **8** on the bottom of this time signature changes the way we interpret the note values. Here's a chart you can refer to:

Clap and count the example below for some practice working in ⁶⁄₈.

Clap:

In ⁶⁄₈ time, the measures are often broken into two groups of three (2 x 3 = 6). Notice that the eighth notes appear either singly ♪ or beamed together in threes. The stresses are usually on beats 1 and 4.

Eighths Beamed in Threes

Here are two examples in ⁶⁄₈.

Try this familiar song in the new time signature.

Oh Dear, What Can the Matter Be?

American Folk Song

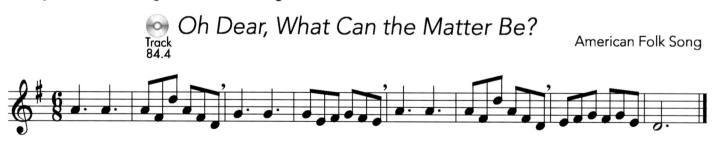

This tune starts with an eighth-note pickup on beat 6.

Vive La Compagnie!

Track 85

Traditional College Song

Count: 6   1 2 3 4 5 6 etc.

Compound Meter

In faster pieces, it becomes impractical to count six beats per measure. In these cases, each measure of $\frac{6}{8}$ is divided into two beats, each worth a dotted quarter note. This means that each beat can be subdivided into three parts. Instead of counting "1-2-3, 4-5-6," we can count "1-&-ah, 2-&-ah." This is called *compound meter*. Time signatures in which the beats are subdivided into two parts, such as $\frac{4}{4}$, $\frac{2}{4}$ and $\frac{3}{4}$, are called *simple meter*. The word "meter" refers to the pattern of beats within a measure. $\frac{6}{8}$ time is a perfect example of why "time signature" and "meter" are not synonymous terms. A slow $\frac{6}{8}$ does not really have the same meter as a fast $\frac{6}{8}$.

For clarification, let's compare the two ways of counting $\frac{6}{8}$.

Counting in "Six"

60

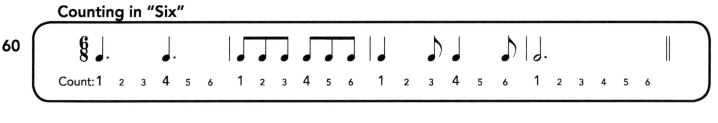

Counting in "Two"

61

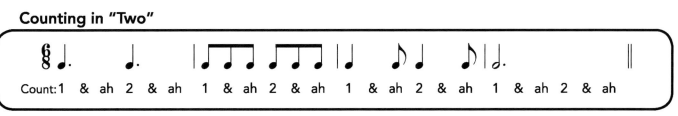

Here's a very familiar tune. See if you can think of it "in two" (and fast!).

Row, Row, Row Your Boat

Track 86

American Traditional

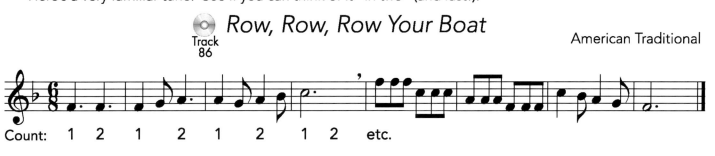

Count: 1   2   1   2   1   2   1   2   etc.

The earliest known written *canon* (round), *Sumer Is Icumen In* dates from about the year 1220. It can be played as a round for five players with entrances two measures apart. Each entry point is marked with an asterisk *. Notice the key signature.

Sumer Is Icumen In

Track 87

Old English Canon

Here's a ⁶⁄₈ piece from the 17th century. Notice the key signature and remember that all Fs and Cs are sharped.

Dargason (or the Hawthorn Tree)

Track 88

English Folk Tune

Here's a quick 16th-century Spanish song.

Pase El Agua, Ma Julieta (Cross Over The Water, My Julieta)

Track 89

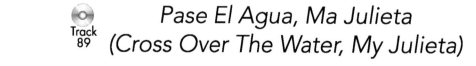

Count: 1   2   1   2   1   2   etc.

Tempo Markings

Tempo markings are used to indicate the speed of the music. There are many tempo markings, but three important ones to know are:

- Allegro   =   Fast
- Moderato   =   Moderately fast
- Andante   =   Moderately slow

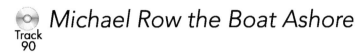

Michael Row the Boat Ashore

Folk Song

Track 90

Notice that the tempo changes in the ninth measure of *The Blue-Tail Fly*.

The Blue-Tail Fly

American Folk Song

Track 91

Composition Exercise #3

Try filling in these incomplete measures. Check the time and key signatures and create a piece you would like to play.

62

63

64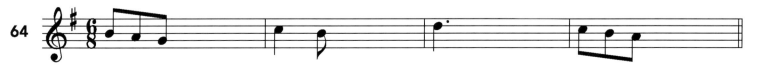

Chapter 6

Introducing High G

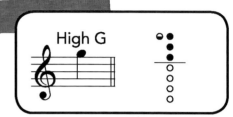

High G is written in the space just above the staff. It's an easy one; just finger low G (page 9), "pinch" the thumb (page 34) and speed up your blowing. Be careful not to over-blow and "crack" the note.

The next two songs use high G, so try them slowly at first

She'll Be Comin' 'round the Mountain

American Folk Song

Track 92

Notice that both sections of *Minuet* repeat.

Minuet

Jacques Hotteterre

Track 93

Ritardando (or *rit.*) is another tempo marking telling you to slow down gradually. It is often found at the end of a piece. Look for it in the New Year's song below.

Auld Lang Syne

Scottish Traditional

Track 94

Candlemas Day

If Can - dle - mas Day___ be fair___ and bright

Win - ter will take___ an - o - - - - ther flight; If

Can - dle - mas Day___ be cloud and rain

Win - ter is gone and will not come a - gain.

Blessings on the candles

Bless-ings on the can - dles That shine in dark-est night

As the stars a - bove, They lead us with their light.

Bless-ings on the Child whose face with love a - glow Brings

strength and truth to us That He our way may show.

Oh Lovely Spring.

R. de Lassus.
J. Wild.

Oh lovely Spring, are all these flowers for

our de- light? The songs of birds and

sweet per- fumes, The nests that are hid - ing

in the woods. And even the silver

moon. a- bove the lake at night?

Here are two more pieces using the high G.

Gavotte
Track 95

Michael Praetorius

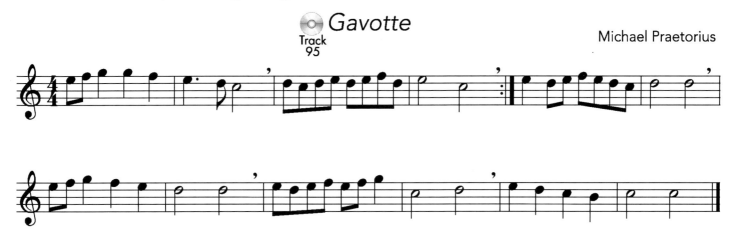

This one is harder. Take it slowly at first. Pay attention to the key signature, the pickup on beat 6 and the slurs.

Kesh Jig
Track 96

Irish Dance Tune

Note Value Quiz

In the right column, write a single note value that equals the combined values of the notes in the left column (assume we are in $\frac{4}{4}$). Each row does not have to equal a full measure. For example, the first row has two quarter notes. Since a quarter note equals one beat, two quarter notes equal two beats. The single note value that equals two beats is a half note, so a half note is written in the right column. The correct answers are upside down at the bottom of the page.

Example: ♩ ♩ = 𝅗𝅥

1) ♩. ♪ = __

2) ♪♩ ♪𝅗𝅥 = __

3) ♫ ♪♩. = __

4) ♩ 𝄽 ♫ = __

Answers: 1) ♩; 2) o; 3) ♩.; 4) ♩.

Cut Time

Cut time ₵ is a time signature that tells you to "cut" the time in half. The half note will get one beat and will be the pulse (beating unit) of the piece. All note values are cut in half (a whole note equals two beats, a quarter note equals half a beat, etc.). Composers usually use cut time to suggest a quicker tempo.

Note and Rest Values in ₵

♪	𝄾	= ¼ beat
♩	𝄽	= ½ beat
♩	▬	= 1 beat
𝅝	▬	= 2 beats

Example 65 demonstrates the difference between cut time and ⁴⁄₄.

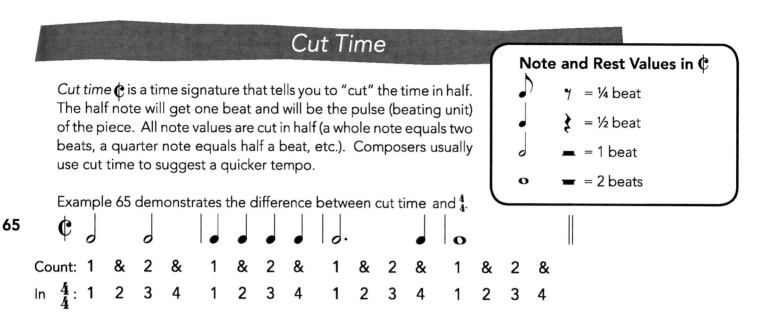

Count: 1 & 2 & 1 & 2 & 1 & 2 & 1 & 2 &
In ⁴⁄₄: 1 2 3 4 1 2 3 4 1 2 3 4 1 2 3 4

The following two pieces are written in cut time. *Canon* was written in the early 16th century.

Canon

Track 97

Thomas Tallis

Moderato

Count: 2 1 2 1 2 etc.

Simple Gifts

Track 98

American Shaker Tune

Allegro

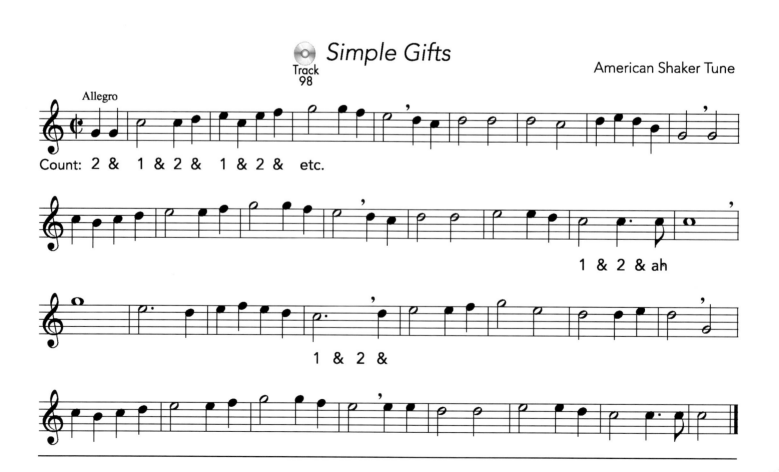

Count: 2 & 1 & 2 & 1 & 2 & etc.

1 & 2 & ah

1 & 2 &

Introducing High F♯

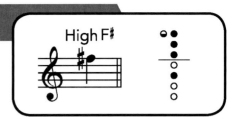

High F♯ is like low F♯ (page 19) with two differences:

1) Only one right-hand finger (middle) is down on a high note.
2) The left thumb, as with high E and above, has to be "pinched" into the thumbhole.

Now that you know high F♯, you can add another scale to your list, the G Major scale. Here's one rhythm in which to play this scale:

The G Major Scale

John Peel

Track 99

American Traditional

Summary of Notes and Scales

Below is a summary of the notes you know. You can also refer to the Fingering Chart on page 47.

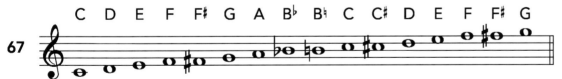

Here are all the scales you have learned:

The C Major Scale

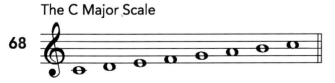

The G Major Scale

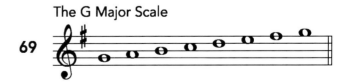

The D Major Scale

The F Major Scale

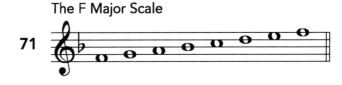

Appendix

The Recorder Family

The recorder comes in nine sizes. As you know, the one you are learning is the soprano, also known as the *descant* recorder. Next larger in size is the *alto* or *treble*, which plays five notes lower than the soprano. Below that is the *tenor*, about twice as long as the soprano, which plays notes an octave lower than the soprano. Though the finger holes are a little further apart on the tenor, the note-names are exactly the same as those on the soprano. The *bass* recorder sounds an octave below (and fingers the same as) the alto.

Those four instruments make up a quartet for which a huge amount of music has been written, especially from the Renaissance period (roughly 1450 to 1600). There is also an enormous catalogue of solo music, largely for the alto recorder, that comes from the Baroque period (approximately 1600 to 1750).

Above and below that family of four instruments, to extend the range of possible notes, are five more sizes. Below the bass is the *great bass*; next comes the *contra*, which stands about six feet tall (and must be played standing). The lowest-sounding recorder is the contra in C (or the *great-great bass*). It is far less common (and also very expensive). At the other extreme, above the soprano, are two more: a *sopranino* and, hardly longer than a pencil, a *garklein* (German for "very small").

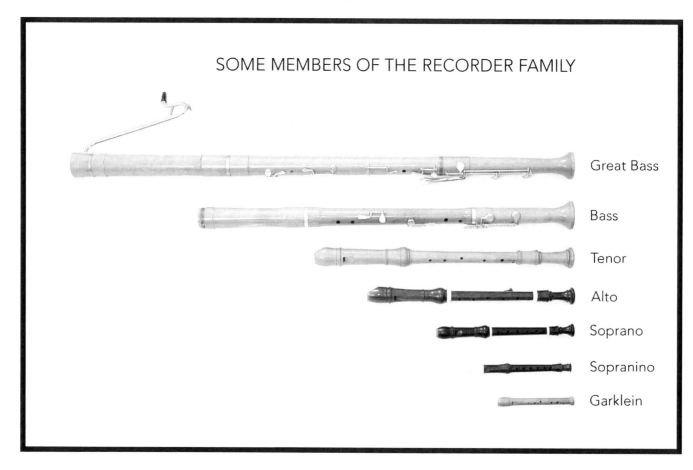

SOME MEMBERS OF THE RECORDER FAMILY

Great Bass

Bass

Tenor

Alto

Soprano

Sopranino

Garklein

Fingering Chart for Soprano, Tenor, Sopranino and Alto Recorder

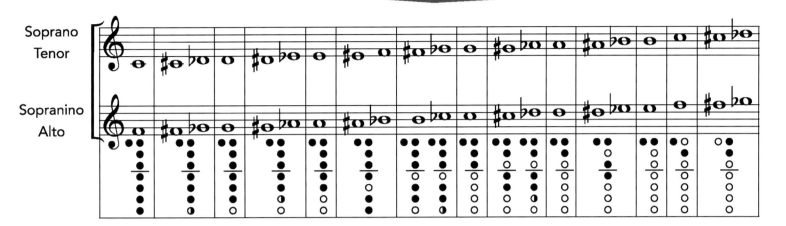

Suggested Supplementary Materials

Now that you have completed *Recorder for Beginners*, here are some places to look for more music:

Basic Recorder Lessons, Book 2, by Ralph Wm. Zeitlin (Amsco Publications)

The Sweet Pipes Recorder Book - Book Two (A Method For Adults and Older Beginners) by Gerald Burakoff, Paul Clark and William E. Hettrick (Sweet Pipes Inc.)

Amazing Solos and Keyboard, selected and arranged by Steve Rosenberg (Boosey and Hawkes Publications)

Elizabethan Music For Recorders, (solos, duets, and trios) by Ralph Wm. Zeitlin (Amsco Publications)

Be sure to play your soprano recorder with other instruments, maybe with a recorder ensemble and also experiment with the other sizes of the recorder family. Enjoy!